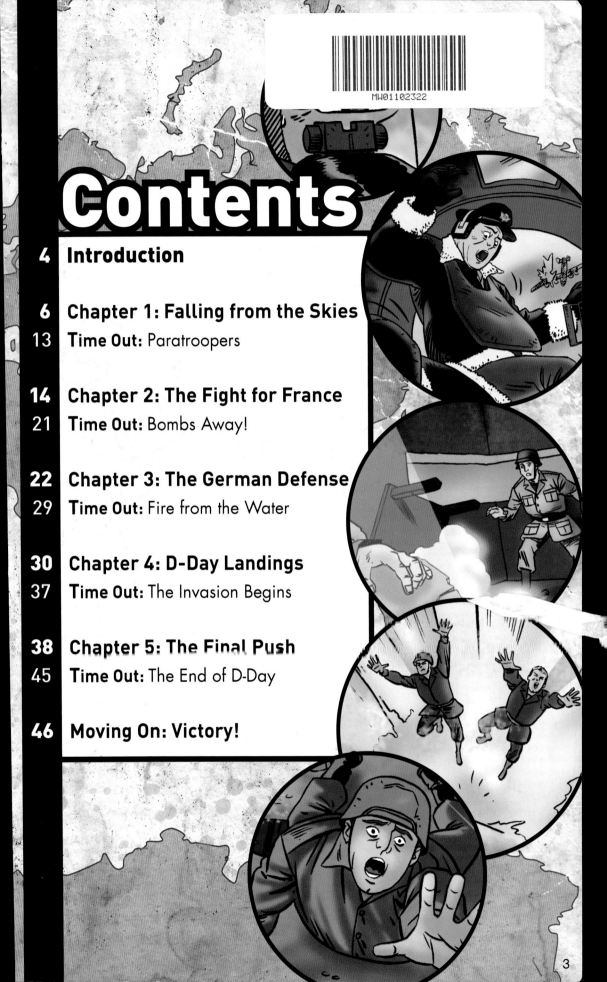

Contents

During the 1930s, Nazi Germany, led by Adolf Hitler, invaded many countries in Europe. Something had to be done! In 1939, Britain and France allied with other nations and went to war against Germany. This was the start of World War II.

In 1940, the Nazis invaded France and held it for four years. The Allies came up with a plan to drive the German army out of France. The plan was called Operation Overlord. It involved a surprise attack on German forces in an area of France called Normandy.

TIMELINE

1933 »	1939 »	1940 »	1941 »
Adolf Hitler becomes chancellor of Germany. He begins to build up the military.	Germany invades Poland. Britain and France declare war on Germany. World War II begins.	Germany invades Belgium, Holland, and France.	Germany occupies Yugoslavia and Greece. Germany attacks Russia. Japan bombs Pearl Harbor, Hawaii.

D-DAY

Written by

ROBERT PIOTROWSKI

Illustrated by

DREW NG

CHARACTERS

MARTIN STEWART

MATTHEW NORRIS

GÜNTHER HERTZ

WILLIAM WARD

JACK HARDY

FICTIONAL CHARACTERS

MARTIN STEWART: A young American paratrooper. He is on an important mission.

MATTHEW NORRIS: A bomb aimer with the British Royal Air Force.

GÜNTHER HERTZ: A young Nazi soldier who fights for his country.

WILLIAM WARD: A young Canadian who lands on the beaches of Normandy.

JACK HARDY: An experienced American lieutenant who leads his men into battle on D-Day.

2

Normandy
Beach

FRANCE

Britain

Netherlands

Belgium

Germany

Switzerland

Italy

Spain

Operation Overlord included armies from Allied nations such as Britain, France, the United States, and Canada. Each had a different role to play in the attack. The Allies knew it would take all of them working together to make Operation Overlord a success.

Allied Supreme Commander Dwight D. Eisenhower decided the surprise attack would take place on June 6, 1944. This date became known as D-Day. This story is about what happened that day ...

WHAT'S THE STORY?

This story is set in an actual time in history and depicts real events, but the characters are fictitious.

1942	1943	1944	May 1945	August 1945
Allied troops, mainly Canadian, are defeated on the French coast at Dieppe.	Allies invade Italy.	June 6: D-Day. Allies land in Normandy, France.	Germany surrenders. Europe celebrates V-E Day (Victory in Europe).	The United States drops atomic bombs on Japan. Japan surrenders, ending World War II.

JUNE 6, 1944: 1:00 A.M. SOMEWHERE OVER NORMANDY, FRANCE ...

AMERICAN TROOPS PREPARE TO PARACHUTE BEHIND ENEMY LINES.

MARTIN STEWART, AN AMERICAN PARATROOPER, PREPARES TO JUMP FROM HIS AIRPLANE.

I DON'T KNOW IF I'M READY FOR THIS.

STEWART JUMPS.

GO! GO! GO!

RELAX. JUST RELAX.

12

PARATROOPERS

In the first part of Operation Overlord, Allied soldiers were secretly sent into France. They jumped from planes wearing parachutes. They were called paratroopers.

Allied paratroopers carried everything from guns to bubble gum and chocolate. Their mission was to surprise the Germans and take control of important areas in Normandy.

Some paratroopers were killed by enemy fire before they even reached the ground. Others became lost and could not find their fellow soldiers. However, the Allied paratroopers and gliders that did land safely behind enemy lines on D-Day managed to weaken the Nazi forces in France.

GENTLEMEN, THIS IS D-DAY!

WHILE AMERICAN PARATROOPERS LAND IN FRANCE, BRITISH AIR CREWS RECEIVE THEIR ORDERS IN ENGLAND.

ALLIED PARATROOPERS HAVE ALREADY LANDED IN FRANCE. NOW WE BEGIN AIR BOMBARDMENT.

FINALLY! LET'S GO!

THE ROOM EXPLODES WITH EXCITEMENT!

BUT, ROYAL AIR FORCE BOMB AIMER MATTHEW NORRIS IS NOT EXCITED.

I'VE HEARD THAT NO BOMBER CREWMAN LIVES PAST HIS 25TH MISSION ...

... AND THIS WILL BE MY 25TH MISSION.

LET'S DROP OUR BOMB LOAD!

THE BOMBS SCREAM AS THEY FALL TO THE GROUND.

CRA-KOOOSH!

THE EARTH SHAKES AS THEY HIT THEIR TARGET.

BOMBS AWAY!

Allied pilots and bomber crews flew over Normandy and dropped bombs on major Nazi gun positions. The idea was to destroy the German defenses from above.

D-Day bomber crews faced many dangers. German anti-aircraft guns fired at them from the ground. Enemy fighter planes guarded the skies.

The weather was stormy and cloudy that morning. Bomber crews had a difficult time figuring out where they were going and when to drop their bombs.

These brave men knew that many of them would lose their lives in the skies over France. Still, they climbed into their planes and took off. Many flew successful missions. Others never returned.

CHAPTER 3: THE GERMAN DEFENSE

JUNE 6, 1944: 5:00 A.M. THE BEACHES OF NORMANDY ARE QUIET — FOR NOW.

A GERMAN SOLDIER NAMED GÜNTHER HERTZ WAITS ANXIOUSLY IN ONE OF THE MANY PILLBOXES THAT LINE THE COAST.

THE ALLIED NAVAL ATTACK COULD START AT ANY MOMENT. I THOUGHT FIGHTING WOULD BE HARD, BUT WAITING IS EVEN HARDER.

I MUSTN'T BE AFRAID. NAZI GERMANY WILL PREVAIL.

FIRE FROM THE WATER

The German army did not expect the Allies to attack Normandy. Hitler and the Nazis were ready for an invasion in another area of France called the Pas-de-Calais.

The Allies knew that invading Normandy would not be easy. They decided to use their navy. There were thousands of Allied ships in the English Channel ready to fire at the beaches on D-Day. The Allies planned to destroy as many enemy defenses as possible before the Allied soldiers began their main invasion.

Germany set up the Atlantic Wall — 3,000 miles of concrete walls, barbed wire fences, and minefields — to protect the coast of Normandy. The Atlantic Wall was packed with heavy guns and German soldiers.

Excerpt from an account written by German gunner Franz Gockel, who was stationed at Omaha Beach on D-Day:

"The bombers were suddenly over us and it was too late to spring into the prepared dugout for cover. I dove under the gun as bombs screamed and hissed into the sand and earth. Two heavy bombs fell on our position, and we held our breath as more explosions fell into the hinterland. Debris and clouds of smoke enveloped us; the earth shook; eyes and nose were filled with dirt, and sand ground between teeth. There was no hope for help ..."

JUNE 6, 1944: AT 7:30 A.M., CANADIAN FORCES PREPARE TO LAND ON JUNO BEACH IN NORMANDY.

ONE OF THE CANADIAN SOLDIERS IN THE ATTACK IS A FARMER NAMED WILLIAM WARD.

I DON'T FEEL WELL. I THINK I'M SEASICK.

WARD, ARE YOU ALL RIGHT?

YOU BET. JUST WATCH ME WHEN I HIT THAT BEACH, BILLINGS. I'M GOING TO BE THE FIRST CANADIAN TO REACH THAT SEA WALL. SINCE YOU'RE MY BEST FRIEND, YOU CAN BE THE SECOND.

WHATEVER YOU SAY, WARD. BUT AREN'T YOU EVEN A LITTLE BIT SCARED?

NO. AND YOU SHOULDN'T BE, EITHER. YOU'LL MAKE IT THROUGH THIS, WAIT AND SEE.

TIME OUT!

Allied soldiers sailed into Normandy to begin the final stage of Operation Overlord. The Allies attacked five different beaches. The Americans landed on two beaches code-named Omaha and Utah. The British attacked two beaches called Sword and Gold. Canadian troops fought on Juno Beach.

Allied soldiers had to fight for their lives on the beaches of Normandy. There were mines in the water and in the sand. Barbed wire and metal spikes lined the beaches. When Allied soldiers got past these dangers, they still had to face the thousands of armed Nazis who were waiting for them.

44

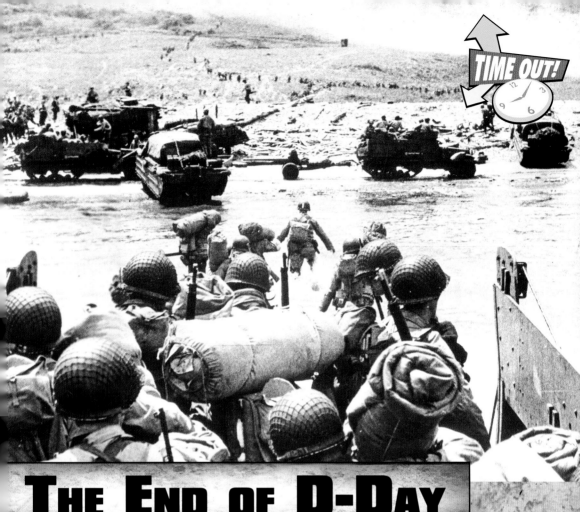

THE END OF D-DAY

Canadian troops were victorious at Juno Beach on D-Day. The British secured Gold and Sword beaches, and the Americans defeated the Nazis at Utah. Omaha Beach was the most difficult to invade. After a long struggle, this area was finally taken.

Many Allied soldiers died on the beaches of Normandy on June 6, 1944. They were soldiers and fathers, brothers, husbands, and friends. They were also heroes. By the end of D-Day, the Allies had secured five beaches in Normandy and landed more than 150,000 soldiers in France. Two months later, they finally took Paris, the French capital, from the Nazis.

D-Day was one of the first in a string of important victories for the Allies. By May 1945, Hitler realized he could not win the war and killed himself. Nazi Germany surrendered a few days later. People in Allied countries celebrated. Europe was finally free from Nazi rule!

With the war over, it was time to undo the harm done by the Nazis. Allied soldiers freed many starving men, women, and children from prison camps. Unfortunately, it was too late for more than six million Jews and millions of others who had died.

Some Nazi leaders who survived the war were captured and punished. The terrible crimes they committed shock the world to this day. They remind everyone that racism and hatred are wrong.

The Allies wanted to make sure nothing like this would ever happen again. They formed the United Nations, an organization that helps keep peace and prevent future wars.

D-Day happened more than 60 years ago, but its effects can still be felt by millions of people today. What would life be like if the Allies had not defeated the Nazis?

Fortunately, the world will never know.

INDEX